Breakout!

The STORY KEEPERS

Episode 1

Breakout!

Brian Brown and Andrew Melrose

ZondervanPublishingHouse

Grand Rapids, Michigan

A Division of HarperCollinsPublishers

Breakout!
Copyright 1996
by Brian Brown and
Andrew Melrose

First published in the UK
by Cassell plc, London

Requests for information
should be addressed to:

Zondervan Publishing House
Grand Rapids, Michigan 49530

ISBN 0-310-20213-2

96 97 98 99 00 01 02 /* XX/
10 9 8 7 6 5 4 3 2 1

Long ago, in the city of Rome,
there lived a mighty ruler.
His name was Nero.
He thought he was a god,
but the Christians knew he wasn't.
So Nero hated them.

One day there was a great fire.
Nero said the Christians started it,
and he sent his cruel soldiers after them.

Marcus, Justin, and Anna
lost their parents during the fire.
Ben the baker and his wife, Helena,
took them into their home.
There, in a time of great danger,
they told the children stories about Jesus.

This book is about the adventures
of the Storykeepers.

"Bread! Freshly baked bread!" Ben shouted.
"Bread for sale," Helena called.

| Ben | Helena | Zak | Justin | Anna | Marcus |

Ben was the best baker in Rome.
Helena was his wife.
Ben and Helena were Christians.
They took care of Zak, Justin, Anna, and Marcus.

The children watched a juggler.
His name was Cyrus.
"How do you do that?" Anna cried.
"Let me show you," said Cyrus.

Anna and Cyrus soon became friends.
"Come to our secret meeting tonight," Anna told Cyrus.
"Ben is going to tell a story about Jesus."

Later that day, Cyrus and the children
went to the secret meeting.
It was dangerous.
The Romans did not want anyone
to tell stories about Jesus.
But Ben loved Jesus.
He wanted to tell the children about him.

"My father was a baker like me,"
Ben told the children.
"One day, I went to hear Jesus preach.
My father gave me a lunch to take with me."

Many people came to hear Jesus.
Over five thousand of them!
Jesus talked to them until it began to get dark.
Everyone was hungry.

"How much food can you find?"
Jesus asked his friends.
"Only five loaves and two fishes," his friends replied.
And they pointed at Ben.

Jesus took the bread and gave thanks to God. Then he broke it into bits, and his friends passed the bread to the people.

Everyone had enough to eat!
They even filled twelve baskets with leftover food.

Suddenly, there was a banging on the door.
It was the soldiers!
"Open up!" they ordered.

"Hurry!" Ben called to the children. Ben, Helena, and the children escaped through a secret exit in the floor.

But Cyrus, the juggler, fell behind. The soldiers caught him and took him away.

The children were very upset.
"We must rescue Cyrus!" they said to Ben.
Ben had an idea.
"We will deliver bread to the prison," he told them.
"Then we will find out where Cyrus is."

Ben, Helena, and
the children found Cyrus.
"There he is!" Anna cried.

"Are you scared, Cyrus?"
Anna asked.
"Yes," Cyrus replied.
"Tomorrow I have to fight
Giganticus. He's huge,
and I am small!"

"Zaccheus was a little man, too,
but he was brave," Helena said.
And she told Cyrus a story
to cheer him up.

Everyone hated Zacchaeus
because he was a tax collector.
He was rich, but did not have any friends.

One day, Zacchaeus heard that Jesus was coming.
Zacchaeus really wanted to see Jesus.
But he was too small.
He climbed a tree so he could see.

Jesus saw Zacchaeus in the tree. "Zacchaeus!" he called. "Come down! I must stay in your house today!"

This made the people angry. "Zacchaeus is a thief and a cheat!" they shouted.

Jesus smiled.
He went to Zacchaeus's house.
He stayed all afternoon.
Zacchaeus was so happy!
"I will give money to the poor,"
he told Jesus. "And I will pay back
all the people I have cheated."

While Stouticus was eating cakes,
Marcus crept up behind him.
He made a print of Stouticus's
key in some dough.
Then Ben and the gang hurried
back to the bakery.

Ben baked a special hard
biscuit in the shape of the key
to Cyrus's cell!

The next day, Ben and Zak returned to the prison.
They took along Ben's special key.
Ben gave cakes to the guards to keep them busy.
And Zak used the key to open Cyrus's cell!

"Follow me," Zak whispered.
He pointed to a door ahead.
Bright sunlight streamed under the door.

Cyrus and the other prisoners followed Zak.
They opened the door.
They blinked in the strong sunlight.
They heard shouting and cheering.

Then they saw him.
Giganticus!
They had walked right into the arena.

"Leave it to me," Cyrus said.
And he began to juggle.
He bounced a helmet
off the giant's head.
The crowd roared.

"Can't catch me!"
Cyrus teased the giant.
Swish! went the huge sword.
Giganticus knocked out Zak.
Then he headed straight
for Cyrus.
"Can't catch me!"
Cyrus laughed.
Giganticus roared with
anger.

No one noticed
Ben opening a gate.
No one saw Justin
climb into a chariot.

The other Christians escaped through the gate.
But Cyrus and Zak were still trapped!

Justin raced up in the chariot.
He grabbed Cyrus and Zak.

And they escaped through the gate,
too.

Back in the bakery, Ben and the children
celebrated with a big dinner.
"Will you stay with us?" Ben asked Cyrus.
He knew Cyrus would not find his parents.

"Oh, may I?" Cyrus cried.
His eyes shone with happiness.
And all the children cheered.

THE STORY KEEPERS

There are thirteen exciting books
in the Storykeepers series.

Episode 1   Breakout!
Episode 2   Raging Waters
Episode 3   Catacomb Rescue
Episode 4   Ready, Aim, Fire!
Episode 5   Sink or Swim
Episode 6   The Starlight Escape

Episodes 7–13
Join Ben and the gang for more
narrow escapes as they fight to keep
the stories of Jesus alive!